Caillou®

As Good as New

Adaptation of the animated series: Sarah Margaret Johanson
Illustrations taken from the animated series and adapted by Eric Sévigny

chouette   COOKIE JAR

Caillou was looking out the
window.
"Daddy, Sarah's riding her bike.
Can we go for a bike ride, too?"
he asked.
"Sure, it's a great day for biking."

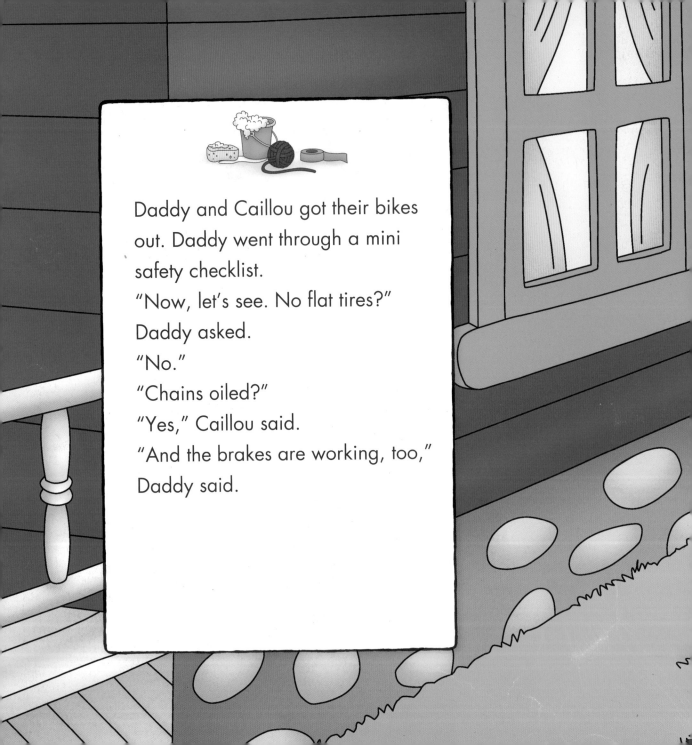

Daddy and Caillou got their bikes
out. Daddy went through a mini
safety checklist.
"Now, let's see. No flat tires?"
Daddy asked.
"No."
"Chains oiled?"
"Yes," Caillou said.
"And the brakes are working, too,"
Daddy said.

Mommy and Rosie came outside.
"We're going bike-riding!" Daddy
shouted.
"That's great. We're going
shopping!" Mommy replied.
Mommy and Rosie drove away.
Caillou and Daddy waved
goodbye from the driveway.

"Hi Leo!"

"Hi Caillou! Look at my new bike!" Leo said.

Caillou was very impressed with Leo's new bike. It had a special flag and streamers.

"Can I ride it?" Caillou asked.

"No, it's my new bike," Leo said.

"I'm sure Caillou would let you ride his bike if you asked him," Leo's mommy said.

Leo let Caillou ride his new bike. Caillou went around the driveway a few times.

"That was fun! Thank you, Leo," Caillou said.

"It's time to go now! Bye!" Leo's mommy said.

Caillou looked at his bike sadly and wished it was as nice as Leo's. "You know, if we clean our bikes they would look as good as new," Daddy said.
So Daddy got a couple of pails of soapy water, and he and Caillou got busy washing their bikes.

"They look brand-new, don't you think?" Daddy asked.

"But Leo has a flag. And steamers, too" Caillou mumbled.

"Those are called streamers," Daddy said. "When I was your age I used to decorate my bike. Would you like to decorate your bike, Caillou?"

"Okay," Caillou replied. He liked the idea of making his bike look special.

Together, they went into the house
to see what they could find to
decorate their bikes.
"How about some red yarn?"
Daddy asked.
"Green too, okay, Daddy? See,
Gilbert likes it too."
Upstairs in Caillou's room, they
found more things.
"These cards are just right, and
this will make a great flag,"
Daddy said.

Daddy and Caillou took everything outside.

They decorated Caillou's bike first.

"Careful now," Daddy said, and flipped Caillou's bike upside down.

Daddy attached a card near the back wheel and spun the wheel.

"That's funny," Caillou said, watching the card flap against the back spokes.

Caillou was having a lot of fun decorating his bike.

Daddy attached the flag to a pole on the back of Caillou's seat. "Wow, your bikes look as good as new!" Mommy said.

"I washed mine all by myself," Caillou said. "Then Daddy helped me decorate it."

"I can see that. There's just one thing missing," Mommy said.

Mommy pulled a bicycle horn out of her shopping bag. She attached the horn to Caillou's bike.
"Wow!" Caillou exclaimed.
Now Caillou really felt proud of his bike.
"Hey, Leo. Come and see my bike!" Caillou said. "Let's go for a ride."

CAILLOU is a registered trademark of Chouette Publishing (1987) Inc.

Text adapted by Sarah Margaret Johanson from the scenario of the CAILLOU animated
film series produced by Cookie Jar Entertainment Inc. (© 1997 Caillou Productions (2004) Inc.,
a subsidiary of Cookie Jar Entertainment Inc.).
All rights reserved.
Original scenario written by Kim Segal.
Original episode no 94: As good as new.
Illustrations taken from the television series CAILLOU and adapted by Eric Sévigny.
Art Direction: Monique Dupras

The PBS KIDS logo is a registered mark of PBS and is used with permission.

We acknowledge the financial support of the Government of Canada through
the Canada Book Fund for our publishing activities.

Canadian Patrimoine
Heritage canadien

We acknowledge the support of the Ministry of Culture and Communications
of Quebec and SODEC for the publication and promotion of this book.

SODEC
Québec

Bibliothèque et Archives nationales du Québec and Library
and Archives Canada cataloguing in publication

Johanson, Sarah Margaret, 1968-
Caillou: as good as new
(Ecology club)
For children age 3 and up.

ISBN 978-2-89450-832-9

1. Salvage (Waste, etc.) - Juvenile literature. 2. Bicycles - Juvenile literature.
I. Sévigny, Eric. II. Title. III. Title: As good as new. IV. Series: Ecology club.

TD792.J632 2012   j363.72'82   C2011-942048-1

Printed in Canada
10 9 8 7 6 5 4 3 2 1 CHO1825 JAN2012

The use of entirely recycled paper
produced locally, containing
chlorine-free 100% post-consumer
content, saved 84 mature trees.